More
NAUGHTY
STORIES
for
GOOD BOYS
AND
GIRLS

CHRISTOPHER MILNE

... A sequel to the very popular
"Naughty Stories for Good Boys and Girls" which in 1992
reached the official Australian Children's Best Seller list.

PUBLISHED BY CHRIS MILNE
C/- POST OFFICE
NEERIM SOUTH   3831

Distributed by E.J. Dwyer/Millenium Books (02) 550 2355

National Library of Australia,
Parkes, A.CT. 2600

ISBN 0 646 10223 0

To
PETE
and
ROB

— CONTENTS —

THE WORST HOLIDAYS EVER

"IF you don't get off your bottom and find something to do I think I'm going to scream," said Belinda's mother. "Such as?" asked a very grumpy-looking Belinda. "Anything!," snapped her mother. "You could help me with the dishes for a start!" Belinda secretly made a very rude sign, stood up and stomped out of the room. "And don't come back till you've wiped that sulky look off your face!" yelled her mother. If Belinda's mother could have seen the sign she made this time, Belinda might not have been able to sit down for a week. Belinda marched into her room and slammed the door behind her.

I guess you could say Belinda and her mum weren't getting along too well. It was near the end of the holidays — the worst holidays ever, thought Belinda — and there was just nothing to do. Nothing! The weather had been terrible — the wettest summer ever, said the lady next door — although Belinda secretly thought the lady next door wouldn't know if a dog bit her. And when it's wet, holidays are just so boring. Belinda had hung around at her friend's so much she thought she might throw up if she had to look at dorky Samantha again. "Gee Samantha is a nerd when you get to know her." In fact, if Belinda really thought about it, all her friends were nerds. And she'd read every stupid magazine and every stupid book that her stupid friends had been stupid enough to buy. When it did stop raining, which was much more often than Belinda would ever admit to, she would go up to the school netball courts. And what did Belinda think of netball now? "Useless! The woosiest game ever invented." Belinda had practised shooting for goals so many times she felt like smashing the ring with an axe. Belinda wasn't a happy girl.

What was even worse was all the lectures she had to put up with from her mother. Especially about Kevin, her boofhead brother: "Why can't you be more like Kevin?" "Kevin is always so good and helpful." "Kevin never has to be asked!"... Kevin is a suck.

So, Belinda lay on her bed and waited. She knew it was only a matter of time before her mother came in with a job for her to do. Smashing the door and being rude always meant jobs. And maybe even a smack. Not that it worried her. At least a smack would be something different. It had been a week.

It's funny how ideas come to you. Why, when you're lying on your bed, really spewing about the worst holidays you'd ever had, would you suddenly think about playing a trick on your wimpy brother? A really nasty trick? Something to do, I guess. And, come to think of it, what about an even worse trick on your bossy mother?

Belinda loved her mum — she wasn't so sure about her brother — and she knew her mum was right when she called Belinda sulky sometimes. But that still didn't mean Belinda liked it. So why not get her mother, too? Suddenly, the holidays were looking better.

First her goody goody brother. Kevin was really into Lego. He had just about every Lego piece ever invented; Pirate, Land, Castle, Space, Technic — you name it. But his favourite was definitely Technic.

Especially the bits that worked with batteries — the lights and motors and stuff.

So, Belinda thought hard. What about flushing his best bits down the toilet? No, somehow that wasn't good enough. What about putting them in the dog's food? That way, if he wanted to get them back he'd have to... No, her mum might make her do it. And then she thought of it! A way of getting her mum and Kevin both at the same time! How excellent!

Belinda quietly opened the door and snuck into Kevin's room. Yes! Everything she needed was there. A big green Lego board and hundreds and hundreds of blocks. Ever so softly she closed the door behind her.

That night, Belinda's mother said how nice it was to see Belinda in a good mood again. And she was very, very pleased to find Belinda had cleaned her room without being asked. Belinda smiled sweetly and like all good girls should, ate up all her vegetables. Who would have guessed that Belinda had secretly planned something terribly, terribly naughty?

After tea, Belinda said to Kevin she was going to her room to do something. "What?" asked Kevin. "Oh, not much," said Belinda. "I might make something for mum. Knit her a scarf or something." Kevin couldn't believe it! Belinda do something for her mother? But the trick worked. What Belinda wanted was for Kevin to make something for his mum, too. Something out of Lego. Belinda knew Kevin couldn't stand the thought of his mum thinking Belinda was a better kid than he was.

So Belinda waited. But she didn't have to wait long. It was only twenty minutes later that Kevin raced out of his room to tell his mum that he'd made her a special surprise. A surprise out of Lego! Quickly Belinda snuck into Kevin's room and smashed his 'surprise' into a thousand bits. Belinda wasn't quite sure what it was supposed to be but she knew it would be something stupid. Very quickly she put something in its place.

Kevin dragged his mum down the passage and proudly led her into his room. And there it was. A poem written in Lego blocks:

GEE I THINK YOU'RE UGLY MUM,

SMELLY BREATH AND BIG FAT BUM.

Belinda just loved the sound of Kevin getting smacked. Something like a wet fish being smashed on concrete. And Belinda especially liked it when Kevin cried so loudly. They were real cries, too. So the smacks must have been good ones. What a perfect trick!

Belinda knew her turn would come. Once her mum found out the truth, she'd be really in for it. But somehow, it didn't matter. At least the holidays had ended well.

Belinda's mum did find out the truth. And Belinda copped the biggest smacking of her life. And that wasn't all. No lollies, no magazines and grounded for a month. But that was OK. It gave her time to think. About even better ways to get her brother. Trouble was, someone else was doing some thinking too. Kevin.

The day after Belinda's punishment finished happened to be her birthday. And secretly and very cleverly, Kevin had decided this would be the perfect day to get his sister back. Belinda had organised a sleep-over party for five of her friends and that usually meant Kevin sleeping on the couch. Just to make sure, Kevin said to Belinda, "There's no way any of your stupid friends are sleeping in my room." Of course, Belinda went straight to her mother and said it was her birthday and Kevin was just being mean and of course her mother agreed. Which was just what Kevin wanted.

That night, Kevin lay on the couch, waiting for his big chance. Finally it arrived. His dad had started snoring and the sound he made was something terrible — like a donkey with clag up its nose. If that didn't make Belinda's friends giggle then they must be asleep. Kevin snuck into Belinda's room, softly pulled back one side of the blankets and poured a glass of water on to her bed. Then he crept into his room, hid behind the door, and started to make some scary, ghosty noises. The two girls sleeping top to tail in his bed woke up straight away and, just as Kevin had hoped, raced out of his room and into bed with Belinda. "Oh, yuck!" he heard one of them say. Kevin tiptoed back to the couch and cacked himself laughing.

In the morning, as the girls sat down to breakfast, there was a poem on the table written in Cornflakes:

I KNOW WHY BELINDA'S RED,

TWELVE YEARS OLD AND
WETS THE BED.

Belinda and Kevin fought like cat and dog over the next few years. One day, however, they just suddenly stopped. No-one knows why — perhaps they both became just too scared of what the other might do next? These days they get along quite well. Sometimes they even talk to each other. Belinda and her mum are O.K. too. Her mother doesn't smack her any more. Somehow, said her mum, it just didn't seem to work. And Belinda's almost forgotten the poem about her mother's bottom. But her mother hasn't. She's been on a diet ever since.

THE BOY WHO PLAYED CRICKET FOR AUSTRALIA

Peter Wallace was mad about cricket. "Cricket Crazy," his dad said. It was cricket this, cricket that. Cricket before school. Cricket after school. If Pete didn't have a bat or ball in his hand his mum used to take his temperature — she thought he must be sick.

Peter wouldn't let his dad and little brother, Robbie, rest for a minute. Always wanting to have a hit in the back yard, always wanting to bat first and never, ever going out L.B.W. Some nights Pete wore his pads to bed. And Rob reckoned on windy, scary nights he wore his protector as well.

As Pete grew older he started to play in an under-thirteens competition. And if anything, his love of cricket became even stronger. And people started to notice something. Pete was becoming a good little player.

But Pete didn't want to be just good. He wanted to play for Australia! It was something he heard on the radio that did it. A young Indian batsman was asked when he first thought about playing for India? "From the moment I picked up a bat," he answered. And Pete thought, "Yes. That's me! I'm not crazy. I want to play for my country too!"

Pete's dad said there was nothing wrong with aiming for the top but not to forget that cricket was just a game. "Play for fun and try your best," said his dad, "And everything else will take care of itself." "Sounds pretty woosy to me," thought Pete, but like a good little boy he just said, "Yes, dad." Pete's dad was always coming out with mushy stuff. "Must have been a bit of a loser when he was young," thought Pete.

And then it happened. The fantastic, unbelievable day of days.

Pete had gone in a muesli bar cricket competition. And won! The prize was a day at a Test Match with Australia playing against the West Indies. But the best part was a chance to go into the Australian dressing rooms before the game. To get all the players' autographs and look at them and stuff. Pete was so excited he thought he might have kittens.

The game was at the most famous place in the world, the Melbourne Cricket Ground, and the newspapers said the place would be packed. And so it was. Lucky they had arrived early. Which was only because of Pete's mum. His dad was always so slow getting ready that his mum said he needed a bomb under him. If he kept them waiting this time they'd go without him. And she meant it. And they did. When Pete's mum got like that his dad got scared of her, so he thought it might be best if he caught the train and met them there. Pete was pleased his mum was nice to his dad in the end, though, because she said, "You can do what you like."

Finally, after waiting in a queue for what seemed like half of Pete's life, they reached the entrance to the Member's Stand. Pete was dressed in his whites and he carried his bat in one hand and his muesli prize letter in the other. And the man at the gate said, "We've been expecting you." Pete felt like a nervous wee but he knew this was no time to ask.

Because players were still getting changed his mum couldn't go in to the dressing rooms so Pete went through by himself. Suddenly, there he was. Surrounded by the most important, fantastic, excellent people ever. The Australian Cricket Team. Alan Border, Merv Hughes, Dean Jones — they were all there. And Pete was introduced to every one of them. He felt like he was in heaven. Mr Border asked if Pete would like to stick around for a while. I don't think I have to tell you what Pete's answer was.

Well, the game had been going for an hour and Australia had started terribly. "Marshy" — that's what Pete calls Geoff Marsh now that he knows him personally — went out for fifteen and Taylor for only twelve. So when Boon went early, too, it looked like disaster.

But the real disaster had only just begun because something else was happening in the dressing rooms that was just awful. Something only Pete knew about. The next two batsmen, Dean Jones and Steve Waugh, who were both supposed to be padding up, were instead being terribly sick in the toilets. It must have been something they'd eaten for breakfast.

Pete was trying to help them by giving them wet towels but they just seemed to get worse. "What are you going to do?" asked Pete. "I don't know," said Jonesy. "Do you think you could run up and tell Mr Border for me? He's in the players' room at the top of the stairs." "Sure," said Pete. "And Pete," said Jonesy, "you've been a terrific help. Thanks. Maybe I can give you a hand one day when you play for Australia?" Pete smiled and ran off. And then he stopped. Those words, "Play for Australia"... And Pete started to think of something very, very naughty.

Pete's mum and dad were together in the grandstand by now and they groaned with the rest of the crowd as yet another wicket fell. Tom Moody. Bowled.

Pete's mum was the first one to notice. "Oh, no!" she said. "It couldn't be!," said his dad. It was. Peter Wallace was marching out to bat.

Mr Border waved madly and shouted at Pete to come back but Pete wouldn't listen. The crowd couldn't believe it. "Who is he?," they asked. "How could someone so little be sent out to bat?" "Why wasn't the team change in this morning's papers?" It was all too late. Pete was at the crease. And Curtly Ambrose was charging in to bowl.

Pete felt pleased that he at least saw the fourth ball he faced. The first three whistled past somewhere near his nose. He knew that because he'd heard them. But the fifth, that was the ball. Pete had decided he was going to have a whack at it no matter what. "Cop this, Curtly," said Pete and bang, the ball rocketed off Pete's bat, over the top of slips, and into the fence for four. The crowd went wild. But the sixth ball thundered into Pete's pads. "How's that!," screamed the West Indies. "Not out," said Pete. Pete was so used to umpiring at home that the words just popped out. The umpire got such a shock he didn't say anything.

And that was the end of the over. Unfortunately it was also the end of Pete. The police had by now found out what had happened and Pete was asked to leave the ground. Pete pleaded to stay a bit longer. Now that he had Curtly beaten he was ready to really cut loose! The policeman shook his head.

So, Pete turned, thanked everyone for coming and proudly marched off the ground. The crowd cheered wildly and Pete lifted his bat in the air like great batsmen do. Just because his magnificent innings had been cut short that was no reason to disappoint the crowd.

That night Pete worked out his Test average. "Four runs divided by no outs equals infinity," said Pete. "But that's a bit unfair. Let's just call it a hundred."

"So why isn't it in all the record books?," I can hear you ask. "And why haven't I even heard of Peter Wallace?" Well, the reason is, the Australian team felt so stupid that Pete had got out onto the ground they asked the West Indies not to count his innings. And the newspapers all agreed not to write anything about it. But I know it happened because I

was there. You see the prize was for two —
Peter Wallace and me, his brother Robbie.
And that's the bit I haven't told you. The best
bit. Because Steve Waugh was sick too, I
came in straight after Pete. And my average is
two hundred.

A VERY LONELY BOY

Little Kenny was a lonely boy. A very lonely boy. He had no friends at all. Unless you count Boof, his dog. No-one could say Boof hadn't been the best dog friend a kid could ever have. But Boof was getting old. And his days of playing with Kenny for hours on end were over. Poor old Boof — he'd see Kenny playing by himself and he knew he should be dropping a stick for Kenny to throw. But his legs just wouldn't take him over any more. If Kenny turned around Boof's eyes would say "stick" and his tail would wag but that was as far as it went. Sometimes it made Kenny cry.

One cold, windy day, Kenny was outside mucking round in the dirt making secret tunnels for some old G.I. Joe soldiers. And much as he tried not to, he started — for what seemed like the thousandth time — to think about why he was such a "loser". That's what Derek "Fierce" Pierce called him, anyway.

He knew that part of the reason was his mum and dad not being together any more, but he didn't want to think about that too much because it made him even sadder. You see, his mum and he had shifted to the country with his grandma, leaving dad in the city. Dad, who he loved so much and now hardly ever saw. At least in the city he'd had one good mate. Stinky Anderson. Stinky had an accident on the first day of school and the name had stuck ever since.

But the biggest reason Kenny was lonely was a feeling that somehow, he never fitted in anywhere. And once you feel that then other kids feel it too. And pretty soon you don't fit in. And then you say, "See, I was right." It was probably because of his mum and dad splitting up. Kenny always secretly blamed himself. It wasn't his fault, of course. It never is. But it made Kenny feel bad about himself and that's when everything seemed to go so wrong. And there was something else — the sort of games Kenny used to like. "Woosy games," some kids would call them. Stuff where you have to think and pretend. Like building dirt castles and having make-believe wars where the bad guys get their heads blown off and guts spurts out of their necks. And collecting lizards and seeing if they die or not. But the other kids in town weren't into dopey stuff like that. They were into grown-up things like cricket and hanging round the milk bar.

Kenny tried cricket in the city. But you'd have to say it wasn't his best sport. Five ducks in a row. The last one was the worst — a run-out. Kenny had finally hit what looked like a single when his protector slipped out the leg of his shorts. Guess who stopped to pick it up? And then he tried tennis. Now, if they started up a new rule which said that instead of hitting the ball you have to let it bounce off your head, Kenny could have been a star, but... And so it went. The things Kenny was good at the other kids thought were boring.

Kenny's mum used to ask kids home to play but somehow they always had excuses. Kenny said it didn't matter because he was really happy being with his mum. And if his mother tried to arrange for Kenny to go to their places, Kenny would say he felt sick. Secretly, he couldn't stand the thought of getting there and not fitting in.

So, Kenny played by himself. Before school, after school, on weekends and on holidays. With sad, smelly Boof looking on. And the wind blew and Kenny's face grew sadder. His beautiful little face. Freckled, with crooked teeth and the loneliest eyes in the world.

Fierce Pierce was the first one to notice. "What do you reckon that loser Kenny's doing in his backyard?" he asked his mate "Fridge". "Every morning when I go past on the way to school there's more dirt. In a pile. Heaps of it." "A swimming pool?" wondered Fridge. Fierce thought not. Surely they'd get a bulldozer or something for that? "Perhaps he's burying food?" thought Fridge. From a stupid suggestion like that you can probably guess how Fridge got his name. Fierce didn't even bother to answer.

So, the very next morning Fierce went straight up to Kenny and said, "Hey loser, what's with all the dirt?" "Oh, nothing," said little Kenny. Kenny would gladly have told Fierce but he thought Fierce might laugh. You see, Kenny was building the most excellent underground cubby house the world had ever seen — for himself and some pretend friends. But how do you admit you're so lonely you have to have pretend friends? "What do you mean, 'nothing'?" said Fierce. Kenny could tell Fierce was going to punch him out if he didn't give a good answer. So he lied. "Mum's making me do it. For pocket money. She's going to plant some trees," said Kenny. Fierce looked hard at Kenny. Fierce knew how cruel parents could be — making you work for pocket money — but he wasn't sure if he believed Kenny or not. But the bell went so Kenny got away with it. For now.

You should have seen the cubby. It started with a secret entrance hidden behind some bushes and then went straight down into a big dark room with candles burning in the corners. Kenny's dad had shown him how to build safe cubbies and somehow, every spadeful of dirt, every heavy bucketful tipped on the pile was for his dad. Maybe one day dad would come to see him again and Kenny could show him what a good job he'd done.

From the main dark room, two tunnels headed off in different directions. If you weren't a member of the cubby club you wouldn't know which was the right one and that was something that definitely needed to be known. One went to the secret chamber, the other to a hole full of the worst, slimiest, stinkiest water you could ever imagine. "Boof's hole," Kenny called it. "Boof's bones and business" hole would have been a better description. Kenny didn't just take Boof's bones, though. He swapped them for big bits of spare steak from mum's fridge. The business came free of charge.

From the secret chamber there were two more tunnels — one leading to the food and drinks cave and the other to a fantastic underground maze. And if you could find your way through the maze — and only cubby members would know how — you finally reached the most secret of secrets — the star chamber. Kenny would never tell what was in the star chamber but to have built such an excellent maze it must have been something good. Really good.

So, the days passed and then weeks and finally, Fierce couldn't help but ask, "Hey, misery guts. What's happened to those trees your mum was putting in?" "She hasn't got them yet," lied Kenny. "I made the holes a bit big so she's got to wait for them to grow." This time Fierce got angry. "Bull," said Fierce. And he pushed him in the chest. "You're lying". "No I'm not," said Kenny. By this time kids were starting to gather around. They loved to watch a fight. Especially if they weren't in it. "Tell me the truth or I'll smash your face in," said Fierce. Given the choice, thought Kenny, he'd rather not have his face smashed in so he took a deep breath and got himself as ready as possible to be laughed at. "It's a secret cubby house," said Kenny. "For me and my friends." "What friends?" asked Fierce. "Pretend ones," said

Kenny. "Pretend ones!" said Fierce. "What a dork! What a loser!" And sure enough, the kids all laughed their heads off. Cacked themselves. But somehow, not for nearly as long as Kenny expected. And, in a strange way, although the kids did laugh a fair bit, Kenny didn't care. At least now it was all over.

But that's where Kenny was wrong. It wasn't all over. Not at all. You see, kids started talking. It was the word "secret" that got them going. As Kenny's mum said, there's nothing country people like better than discovering a good secret.

And then the rumours started. One rumour said that Kenny was building a huge grave for Boof — what with Boof looking like he was going to cark it any day now. Another said Kenny was working as a spy and it was really an underground nuclear reactor. Whatever it was, almost every kid in school decided he just had to know.

So, one night after school, Fierce and twenty-six of his mates knocked on Kenny's door and said if Kenny didn't show them his cubby they'd bash his brains out. Luckily, Kenny's mum was listening so she went to the door and said, "You must be Fierce?" "Yeah," said Fierce. "So what?" "So why don't you all come inside?" said Kenny's mum. "I've got so many boxes of chocolate left over from Easter and plenty of lemonade in the fridge. No point in bashing Kenny's brains out on an empty stomach." Fierce was so surprised by what Kenny's mum said that suddenly all his toughness just seemed to leave him. "O.K." said Fierce. "Thanks." So, including Kenny, twenty-seven kids sat down and gutsed themselves sick. After that no-one felt like bashing anyone's brains out. And slowly and strangely, Kenny started to feel good. It mightn't be for the best of reasons, but for the first time in so long he didn't feel lonely.

And then the suggestions started. "Hey, Kenny," said one kid. "How 'bout we have a muck around in your cubby?" "Sure," said Kenny, "But parts of it are dangerous, very dangerous, so I'd better show you a map first.

And to be allowed in at all, you have to be a member. Do you all want to join?" "Yeah!" they all shouted. So, quietly and carefully, Kenny showed the kids how to pick the right tunnels, how not to fall into Boof's hole and how to get through the maze to the secret of secrets — the star chamber. And everyone loved it. Somehow, because Kenny had been lonely for so long and because he'd had to use his imagination so much, Kenny had found a way of making things sound exciting. Really exciting. It wasn't so much what he said but the way he said it. Even Fierce secretly thought to himself he could just sit there and listen to Kenny for ever. There was this look in Kenny's eyes which made it seem as though he knew things they could never know — as though he'd been to a place they never even knew existed. And when Kenny said, "O.K., is everyone ready?," kids just sat there and waited for him to say something else. Never in their lives had they realised that telling stories and stuff could be so much fun. Almost as good as mud fights.

Fierce and his mates thought the cubby was so excellent. "Radical," they said. And somehow, from that day on, Kenny just knew he would never be without friends again. Because the kids had come to him. They had fitted in with him. Well, not fitted in, exactly. It was just that everything felt O.K. And if you feel O.K. making friends is easy.

Now, what was or wasn't in the star chamber will never be known because only members were allowed in. And one of the rules of membership was keeping things secret. At one time a rumour went around Kenny had discovered gold down there and that he would wait till he was older so the government didn't take it. Who knows, could be true.

As little Kenny watched his new friends playing in the cubby one day, he walked over to the spot where he used to play G.I. Joes. He smiled and he thought to himself he had never felt happier in his life. He was even going down to see his dad every second weekend. He also felt something else.

Something furry. It was Boof, with his tail wagging, eyes shining and looking younger than he had for years. With a big, wet stick in his mouth.

THE BEST PLACE IN THE WORLD

There were lots of good things about living in Neerim West. "In fact," thought Brett Porter and his brother, Dave, "it's probably the best place to live in the world." They could easily ride their bikes to the lolly shop, there was a really excellent creek running right through their farm and best of all, the Neerim West Tip was right next door.

Not only was the Neerim West Tip good for normal rubbish, everybody dumped their old cars there as well. And sometimes, if the scouts didn't get there first, there were full bags of bottles to smash.

Dave and Brett liked the smell best. Somehow, the mixture of rotting food, old tyres and dead cats made a smell which said "excitement". Who knows what you might find? Maybe an old radio with lots of wires and stuff, kids' toys, comics. Even a half-eaten toffee apple, once. Dave had a lick but he reckoned it tasted a bit like fishguts.

The best fun of all was checking out the old cars. Brett and Dave always started by smashing out the windows. Brett really liked front windscreens because sometimes he'd get two shots. First a small rock to make a hole. And then a brick to finish it off. Once inside the cars they'd muck around for hours. Dad was always yelling at them for being late home for tea.

One day, Brett was fooling around in the back seat of an old Ford and he had this really dreamy look. "Wouldn't it be excellent," said Brett, "if we could get one of these cars going one day?" "You serious?" asked Dave. "Dad would kill us." "Not to drive, stupid, just to rev the guts out of it," said Brett. "And maybe make a machine or something." "Oh," said Dave. "What sort of machine?" "Oh, I dunno. A pretend helicopter or something," said Brett. But Dave could tell Brett wasn't thinking "pretend" anything. You see, sometimes, Brett could be very, very naughty.

And from that day on, Brett started to really check the cars out. And Dave helped him. Poor Dave — he knew Brett was thinking something naughty but what could he do? Brett was his brother! His older brother. The best brother a kid could ever have. Brett knew heaps about engines from helping his dad fix the tractor all the time. Well, sort of help. His dad would have called it getting in the way. Brett reckoned that if some of the cars only had little things wrong with them then maybe he could take the best bits from lots of cars and build a new one. A car that actually went. It made him excited just to think about it.

So, for the next four weeks, every night after school, Dave, and Brett went through every old car they could find. It wasn't too hard getting the bits because they borrowed dad's best tools. They didn't tell their dad but it wouldn't have mattered because their dad had boxes of them.

You should have seen all the bits Brett and Dave found. Enough for six engines. "Well," said Brett, "I say we connect it all together and just see what happens". "Fair enough," said Dave. So, they bent and screwed and lifted and twisted and if something didn't fit they hit it. Softly at first and then really hard with a lump of steel. A couple of things smashed into a thousand bits but that was O.K. They were having terrific fun and it had been really hot so the tip smelt great.

Finally, there it stood. The... Well, what could you call it? The "thing". There were bits of pipe and wires and batteries and pieces of engine all over the place. And two huge pieces of pipe tied together on top like a helicopter's propeller. "You ready?" said Brett. "What for?" asked Dave. "To hop in and see if it starts," said Brett. "Hop in?!" said Dave. "It might explode!" "No way. Trust me," said Brett. Dave always knew that whenever Brett said, "Trust me" something bad was going to happen.

Brett took a deep breath, leant forward and pressed the starter button. Nothing. Dave felt like shouting "Hooray," he was so relieved. But Brett pressed the button again. "Oh no!" said Brett. "I think I heard something." Although Brett wanted it to start he sort of didn't at the same time. He was excited but secretly scared as well. He pressed it again. This time a louder sound. A much louder sound. The sound of an engine starting. And the sound of helicopter blades going round. "Oh no!" said Brett again. But this time he really meant it. Dave's eyes were almost popping out.

"Brett!" screamed Dave. "I think we're moving. I think we're moving up!" And they were. This was no pretend helicopter. Brett and Dave Porter were flying.

"Don't panic," said Brett. "Dad always says not to panic." Dave had never been really sure what "panic" meant. And right now he didn't care. He was too busy wishing he'd been to the toilet. Brett pushed and pressed at every lever he could find but they just kept going up. "Make it stop," screamed Dave. But Brett didn't know how.

"Hang on," said Brett. "I've found something!" If I push this lever we go sideways... And if I push this one we go forward." "Just find one to go down! Please!" yelled Dave. "I'm trying," said Brett. "But I can't. We're just going to have to stay up here till the petrol runs out." Dave needed to go to the toilet now for two reasons. He was going to be sick.

But someone else was starting to feel better. Much better. Brett Porter, ace helicopter pilot.

Brett leant forward and with a crazy look in his eyes pushed a lever which he knew would make the engine go faster. Much faster. "Hang on, Davey boy," said Brett. "We're going for a spin."

Meanwhile, Mr Porter was having a lovely day. The sun was shining, he was driving his favourite tractor and the birds were singing. And the birds were flying about, too. Big birds. In fact, one very big bird. Make that a huge bird. Headed straight at him! "Oh, no," shouted Mr Porter. "A space ship!" He flung himself under the tractor, waited till it had whooshed past, then raced inside.

Brett was cacking himself laughing so much he almost crashed into a tree. And then, splutter, cough and the engine stopped. As quickly as the ride had started it was over. Now, if you've ever seen a rock fall from the edge of a cliff you'll have some idea of how quickly their fabulous flying machine dropped into the middle of dad's dam. Never to be seen again. Luckily Brett and Dave were to be seen again. Sore, wet and very sorry.

As they walked slowly back to the house their dad rushed up to tell them the news. He didn't even notice they were wet. "You'll never guess," said their dad. "I just saw a flying saucer." "Really?" said Brett. "Who was flying it?" "Creatures from outer space," said dad. "Ugly looking things."

That night, Brett and Dave told their dad the truth. Their dad said that telling the truth was always best because you don't you have to carry the lies around with you forever. He always punished them. But at least they knew it was over. Then they could start fresh and do something else naughty.

Their punishment was hard, but probably fair. No playing at the tip for a year and jobs every night after school picking up potatoes for no money for six weeks. And Brett said a big sorry to Dave. It was all his fault, he said. They could have been killed! Dave said not to worry. They're brothers aren't they? Mates. All the same, Dave wished Brett would stop his latest hobby of buying "Do It Yourself" books. Especially one called "Submarines for Two".